# THE BURP

## THAT SAVED THE WORLD

POPPO

POP 'TIL YOU DROP!

# THE BU

For Caniad.

With thanks to Jo Beggs, Kate Shaw, Jane Buckley,
Lara Hancock, Ygraine Cadlock & Maxine Lee-Mackie.
MG

For Irene, Ella and Lydia who are most definitely NOT burping twerps.

Thanks to Jane Buckley for tremendous art direction, Mark Griffiths
for a brilliant story and Shaun, Luca and Emilio for their help and support.
ML

SIMON AND SCHUSTER
First published in Great Britain in 2015 by Simon and Schuster UK Ltd, 1st Floor, 222 Gray's Inn Road, London WC1X 8HB
ISBN: 978-1-4711-2479-2 (PB) • ISBN: 978-1-4711-2480-8 (eBook) • 10 9 8 7 6 5 4 3 2 1

# RP

# THAT SAVED THE WORLD

## MARK GRIFFITHS

## ILLUSTRATED BY MAXINE LEE-MACKIE

SIMON AND SCHUSTER
London   New York   Sydney   Toronto   New Delhi

Let's hear about the Mustard twins,
a pair of dreadful twerps,
whose names were known throughout the land

for doing horrid

**BURPS!**

THE DAILY BUZZ

MUSTARD TWINS IN WINDY SHOCKER

One **BURP**
could stun a rhino.

Two could fell an old oak tree.

Young Ben and Matt could shatter glass
if they **BURPED** in harmony.

They **BURPED** in quiet libraries,

and at country summer fetes.

They **BULGED** at waiters in cafes

and made them drop their plates!

The townsfolk grew so weary
of this **BURP**-producing pair,

that they wrote the twins a letter
ordering them to move elsewhere.

Dear Mustard Twins,
Go away!
Yours sincerely,
Everyone x

The twins exchanged a saddened look
and packed their old suitcases.

But then a look of shocked surprise
spread over their two faces.

For in the sky there now appeared
a most alarming sight . . .

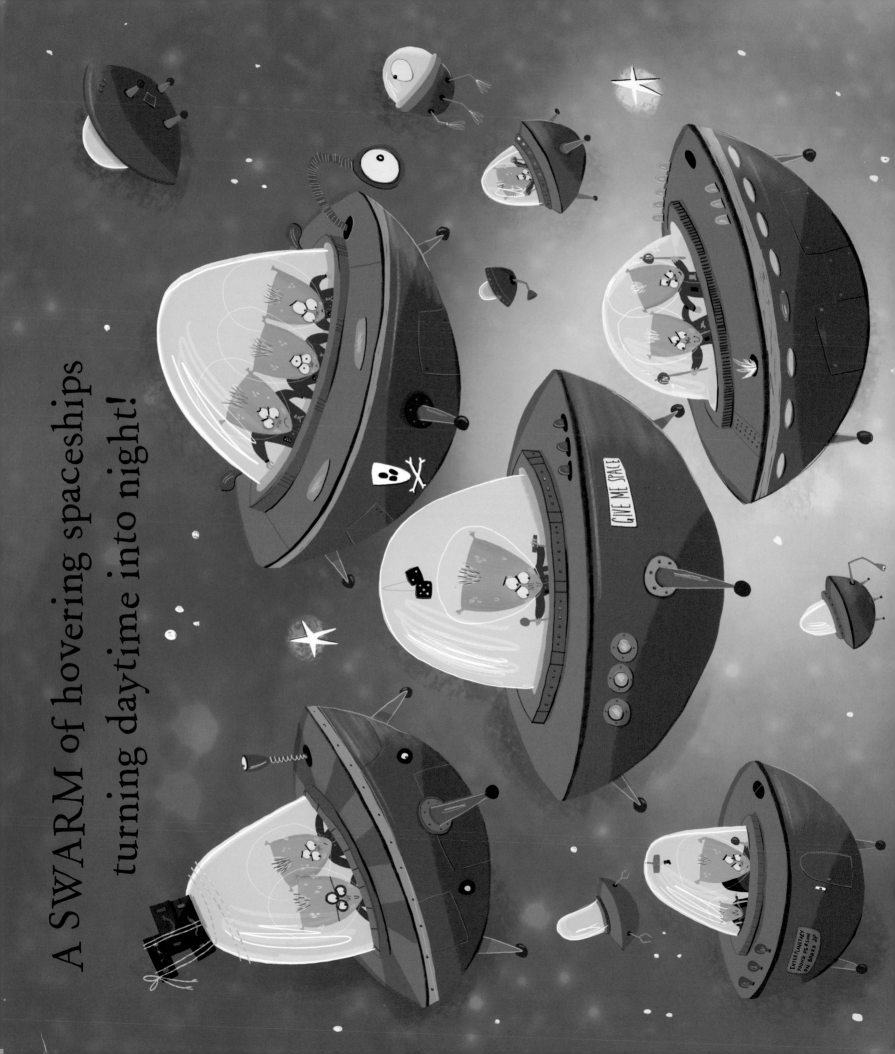

A SWARM of hovering spaceships turning daytime into night!

This fleet of flying saucers
came from far off outer space

and the ugly beings inside them
did NOT like the human race.

"WE'VE COME TO RAID YOUR PLANET!"
cried the leader of these creeps.

"GO FETCH US ALL YOUR CHILDREN'S TOYS

AND PILE THEM UP IN HEAPS."

The frightened people piled up toys
in parks,

in shops,

SWEETS

in streets.

And the ZOOMING flying saucers
scooped them up like tasty sweets.

The army and the navy tried to fight
these alien raiders,

but all firepower was useless against these
TOY-THIEVING INVADERS.

"It looks like we are finished!"
came the cry across the land.

"Is there no one who can save us
from this fiendish alien band?"

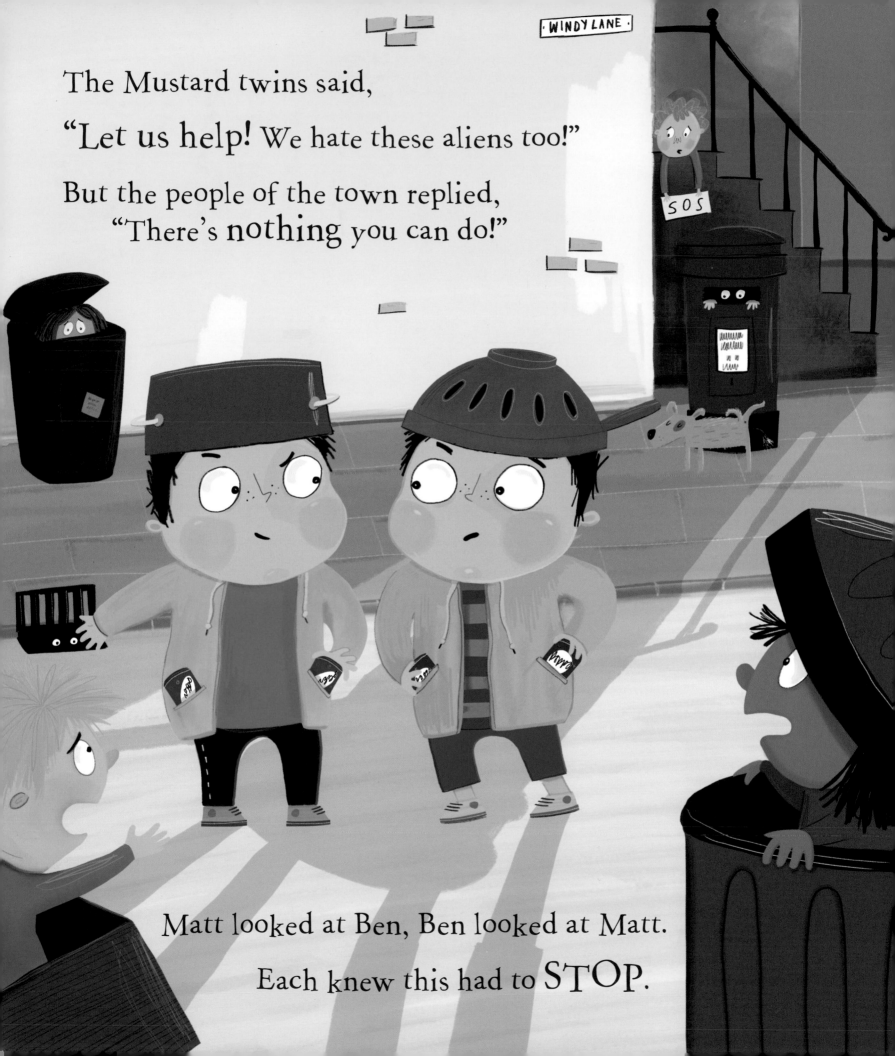

The Mustard twins said,

"Let us help! We hate these aliens too!"

But the people of the town replied,
    "There's **nothing** you can do!"

Matt looked at Ben, Ben looked at Matt.

Each knew this had to STOP.

And from the pockets of their coats
produced two cans of pop.

They shook the cans and pulled the rings,
the pop was sweet and fizzy.

They drained their drinks to the last drop and said,

"Right, let's get busy!"

The two twins opened wide their mouths
and out came such a wonder.

The biggest burp you ever heard
far louder than mere thunder –

It SHATTERED nearby window panes

and FRIGHTENED cows on farms.

It set off minor EARTHQUAKES

and a THOUSAND car alarms.

It scared the aliens half to death,
it was more than they could stand –

as the foulest **BURP** in the universe
rang out across the land.

The loudest **BURP** in history!
Real stomach-turning stuff.

"NO MORE!" the alien boss declared.

"I THINK WE'VE HAD ENOUGH."

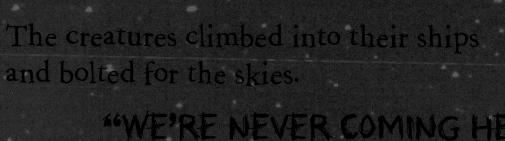

The creatures climbed into their ships
and bolted for the skies.

"WE'RE NEVER COMING HERE AGAIN!"
they sobbed with tear-streaked eyes.

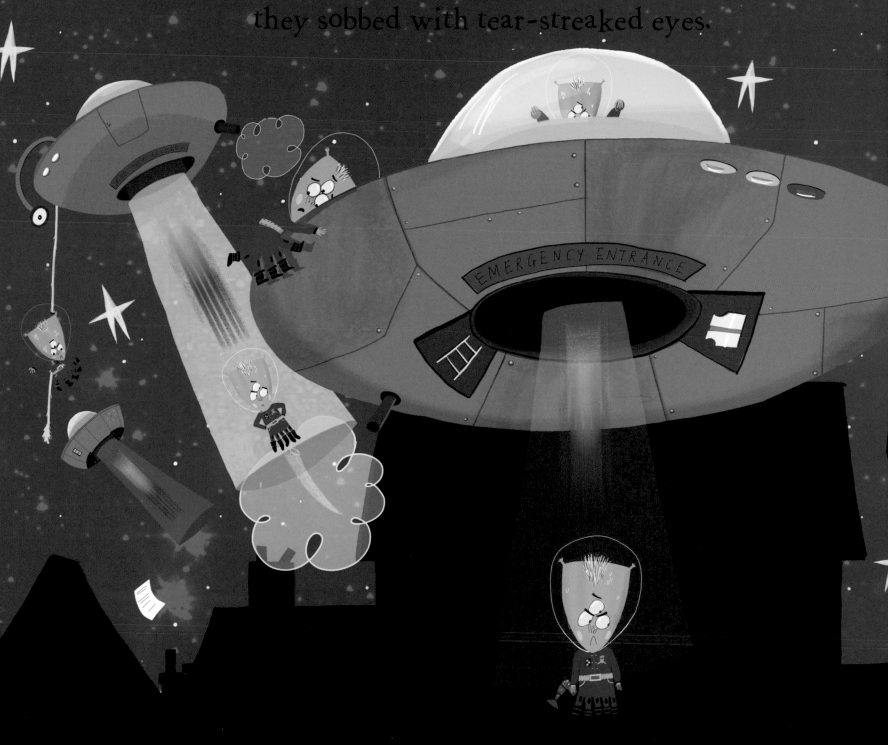

"Hurray! The planet Earth is safe!" the townsfolk told the twerps.

"We owe it all to Matt and Ben – and their tremendous **BURP!**"

The twins were given medals
at a party on the green.

They lifted high their cans of pop
and **BURPED . . .**